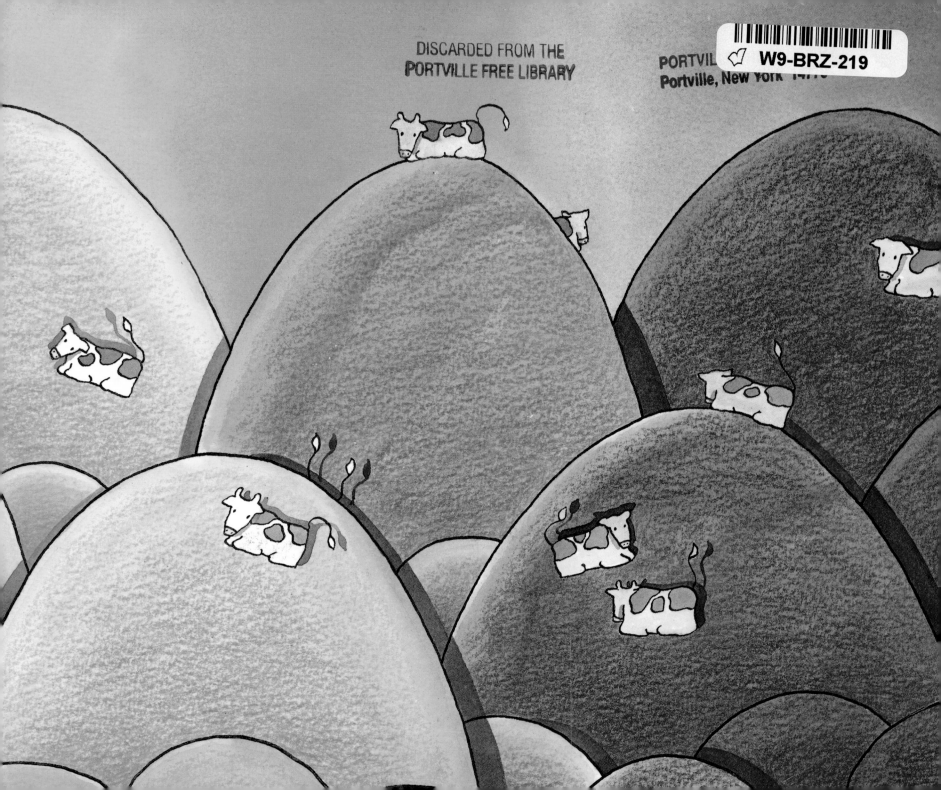

For Susie, with all my love

Published by Clarkson N. Potter Inc., 201 East 50th Street, New York, New York, 10022 and distributed by Crown Publishers Inc.

First published in Great Britain 1991 by ABC, **All Books for Children**, a division of The All Children's Company Ltd 33 Museum Street, London WC1A 1LD

CLARKSON N. POTTER, POTTER and colophon are trademarks of Clarkson N. Potter, Inc.

Library of Congress Cataloging-in-Publication Data

McAllister, Angela
The battle of Sir Cob and Sir Filbert / Angela McAllister
    p. cm.
Summary: Sir Cob and Sir Filbert battle over territory until each makes a discovery about sharing.
[1. Sharing–Fiction.]   I. Title
PZ7.M47825Bat 1991
[E]–dc20   91-19023
                                                                          CIP
                                                                          AC

Manufactured in Hong Kong.

ISBN: 0-517-58730-0

10 9 8 7 6 5 4 3 2 1

First American Edition

THE BATTLE OF SIR COB AND SIR FILBERT

ANGELA McALLISTER

Clarkson Potter/Publishers NEW YORK

This is the story of
Sir Cob and Sir Filbert.

One morning Sir Cob looked out from his battlements. "I have so many things, I need more room," he said. "That castle looks bigger than mine."

And Sir Filbert looked out from his parapet. "I have so many things, I need more room," he said. "That castle looks bigger than mine."

So they prepared
to do battle.

"I must have your castle, Sir!" they said.

"Let the battle commence!"

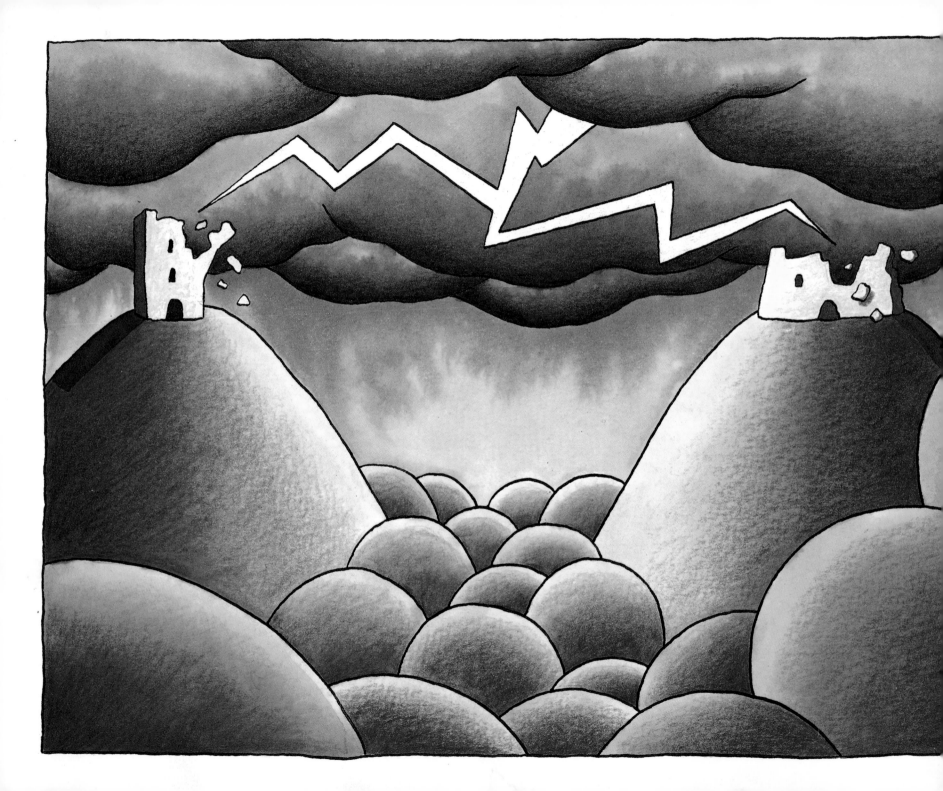

First they fired their bun-blasters...

...then they swung their thwackarees...

...then they charged with their pikeypokes.

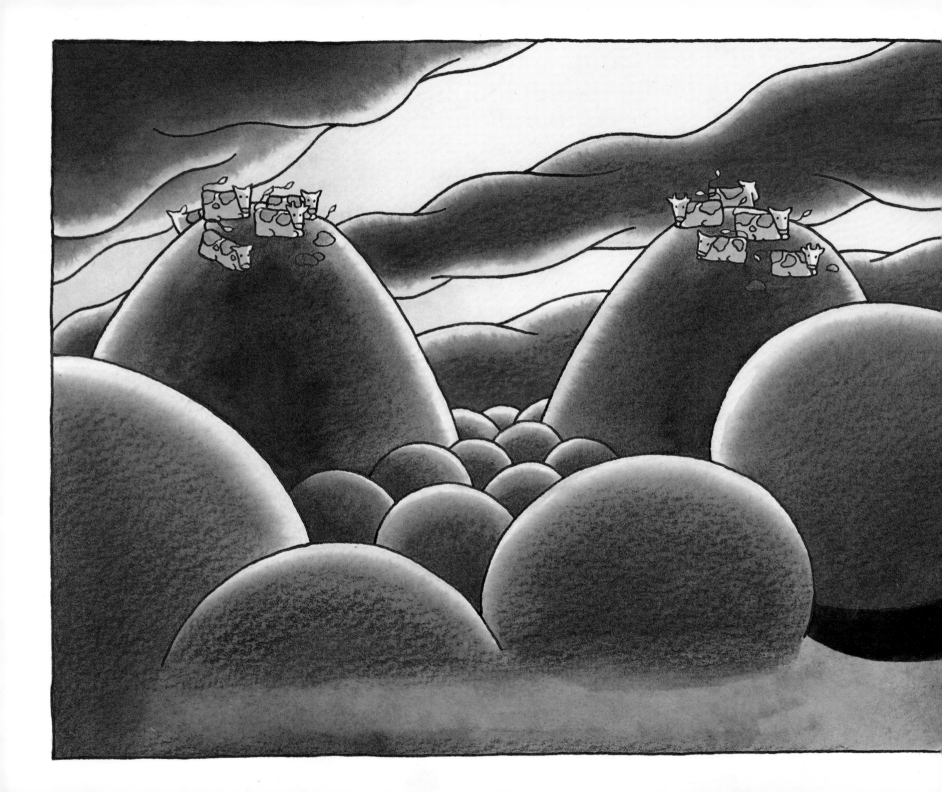

They swiped with their conker-bonkers until...

They saw only cows where
their castles had been.
"Well, we don't need much
room anymore," they said.
"We have nothing left!"

"Let's build a new
castle," they said.
"We'll live there together
and always be friends."